To the consonants
—Dave

To the vowels
—Jim

You guys have always been there for us.

Henry Holt and Company, LLC, Publishers since 1866
175 Fifth Avenue, New York, New York 10010
mackids.com

Library of Congress Cataloging-in-Publication Data
Tobin, James.
The very inappropriate word / Jim Tobin ; illustrated by Dave Coverly. — 1st ed.
p.   cm.
Summary: Michael loves collecting words, especially those that are unusual, and knowing that
one of his new words is naughty does not stop him from sharing it with his friends at school.
ISBN 978-0-8050-9474-9 (hardcover)
[1. Vocabulary—Fiction. 2. Swearing—Fiction. 3. Schools—Fiction.] I. Coverly, Dave, ill. II. Title.
PZ7.T56152Ver 2013 [E]—dc23 2012021084

First Edition—2013 / Designed by April Ward
The artist used ink and watercolors on Arches 90-pound hot-press
watercolor paper to create the illustrations for this book.

Printed in China by Toppan Leefung Printing Ltd., Dongguan City, Guangdong Province
1 3 5 7 9 10 8 6 4 2

The Very Inappropriate Word

FLING

Jim Tobin • illustrated by Dave Coverly

Christy Ottaviano Books

Henry Holt and Company ◎ New York

Michael collected words.

edium (*mee-dee-uhm*)

1. *adjective* – the size between large and small
2. *noun* – a person who believes he or she can communicate with the supernatural
3. *noun* – Grande (*Starbucks*)

edley (*med-lee*)

1. *noun* – a piece of music that combines passages from different sources
2. *noun* – a variety of vegetables mixed together
3. *noun* – a piece of music about a variety of vegetables mixed together

eek (*meek*)

1. *adjective* – shy or submissive
2. *noun* – people who shall inherit the earth, so perhaps you'd better be nice to them

eet (*meet*)

1. *noun* – a race or other competitive event, such as track or swim
2. *verb* – when adults in business attire gather around a long table at work for hours to make a decision that one person could have made alone in minutes

egaton (*meg-uh-tuhn*)

1. *noun* – a unit of explosive power equal to one million tons of TNT
2. *noun* – the amount of trouble you may get in if your grandmother tells your mom she heard you using a very inappropriate word

elancholy (*mel-uhn-kol-ee*)

1. *noun* – a prolonged and gloomy state of mind, often triggered by too much homework and not enough ice cream

ellow (*mel-o*)

1. *adjective* – soft and flavorful from ripeness
2. *adjective* – easygoing or relaxed
3. *adjective* – the sound of that horrible music your parents hum along to in the car

embrane (*mem-brayn*)

1. *noun* – a thin layer of animal or vegetable tissue that lines an organ or connects parts
2. *noun* – the thing that controls the membody

erit (*mer-it*)

1. *noun* – something that has value
2. *noun* – a good point
3. *verb* – to deserve praise; see *Children's Book Editor*

ermaid (*mur-mayd*)

1. *noun* – a mythical sea creature with the lower body of a fish and the upper body of a woman; tends to sing well in Disney movies, even underwater

erry (*mer-ee*)

1. *adjective* – happy and cheerful
2. *noun* – male backup singers in Robin Hood's band

erry-go-round (*mer-ee-go-rownd*)

1. *noun* – a revolving ride at fairs generally consisting of fake horses, intended for the amusement of those under the age of ten or people with a very low threshold for amusement in general

mesa (*may-suh*)

1. *noun* – a large, steep hill with a flat top, like a military haircut but less fuzzy

mesh (*mesh*)

1. *verb* – to fit together
2. *noun* – material made of woven thread, used in those unfortunate tank tops common in the 1970s

mess (*mess*)

1. *noun* – a problematic situation
2. *noun* – something dirty or unkempt (*unkempt*: something dirty or a mess)
3. *verb* – (mess up) to make something dirty or, you know, unkempt

message (*mes-ij*)

1. *noun* – information intended for someone; often found in a bottle sent from a desert island
2. *noun* – the meaning of something said or written; e.g., "The author's message said you should not believe everything you read"

messenger (*mes-uhn-jur*)

1. *noun* – a person who delivers messages
2. *noun* – a person who should not be shot

messy (*mes-ee*)

1. *adjective* – not clean or tidy; see *teenager's room*

metabolism (*muh-tab-uh-liz-uhm*)

1. *noun* – the body's process of changing food into energy, which doesn't work as well if all you eat is junk food, so eat your fruit and vegetable medleys

metal (*meh-tuhl*)

1. *noun* – a material that is generally hard and shiny, such as gold and silver
2. *adjective* – a type of music, usually played very loudly by screaming men dressed in black who have big hair

metallic (*meh-tal-ick*)

1. *adjective* – made of metal, or something that seems made of metal, like the fake armor actors wear when making a movie because if that stuff was real armor, the actors would sweat a lot and it would be difficult for them to use the bathroom

metamorphosis (*met-uh-mor-fuh-sis*)

1. *noun* – the change that certain animals go through as they develop into adults; a good example is the caterpillar, which cocoons itself, grows some wings, and leaves its cocoon as a giant, bloodthirsty bat. Or a butterfly. Usually a butterfly. But wouldn't caterpillar bats be cool?

metaphor (*met-uh-for*)

1. *noun* – a word or words used to compare two different things that have similar features, such as "This definition is a very organized bowl of alphabet soup"

meter (*mee-ter*)

1. *noun* – a unit of measure in the metric system equaling about 39.37 inches
2. *noun* – an arrangement of words in rhythmic verses, making poems sound better but sometimes much worses

He found lots of
words on signs

and a few on TV.

He picked up new words at practice

and downtown

and even in school,
where Mrs. Dixon gave the kids
one new spelling word every day.

He especially liked
little words for big things

and big words for little things

and easy words for hard things

and hard words for soft things.

Every night, he took all his words home and put them in a box under his bed.

One morning on the bus,
Michael picked up a word
he had never heard before.

When everybody was off the bus, Michael's sister said, "Michael! That is a very inappropriate word!"

"What does 'inappropriate' mean?"
Michael asked his friend.

"Bad!" whispered his friend.

So Michael hid the word
in his pocket.

That afternoon, Michael heard the word at the park

and on the radio

and even in the basement, where his mom was trying to fix the toilet.

"Dear!" said his dad. "Don't you think that's an inappropriate word?"

Michael could see there was something kind of bad about it. But there was also something about it that he kind of liked.

The next day at recess, he showed the word to his friends.

"It's BAD!" he whispered.

Scott tried the word out loud. Sharon tried it louder.

Then Michael yelled it at the top of his lungs.
"Michael!" said the recess supervisor.
"That is a very inappropriate word!"

By lunchtime, a few other people were saying the word.

Then, in class, it seemed like everybody was saying it.

"Class!" said Mrs. Dixon. "Where did that word come from?"

"MICHAEL!"

"I see," said Mrs. Dixon. "Michael, please see me after school."

Finally, the bell rang.

"Michael,"
said Mrs. Dixon.

"Michael,
Michael,
Michael.

I need a little help
in the library."

"I'll try," said Michael.

Michael found...

words underwater — SNORKEL

words in the sky — NIMBUS

words underground — LAVA

words that spy — SLEUTH

words that fight — QUARREL QUIBBLE

words that sing — VIBRATO

words for doing crazy things — SHENANIGANS

Michael dug up new words for two hours and forty-five minutes. Then Mrs. Dixon said, "Thank you, Michael. That's enough for today."

"Okay, Mrs. D.," said Michael. "But is it all right if I take a couple of these words home with me?"

"Sure," said Mrs. D.

Michael had so many new words that he lost track of the very inappropriate word.

So, of course, somebody else picked it up.